# Leaf Dance

For Mom and Dad—B.P.

LITTLE SIMON
An imprint of Simon & Schuster Children's Publishing Division
1230 Avenue of the Americas
New York, New York 10020
Text and illustrations copyright © 2001 by Simon & Schuster, Inc.
The names and depictions of Raggedy Ann and Raggedy Andy are trademarks of Simon & Schuster.
Manufactured in the United States of America
First Edition
2  4  6  8  10  9  7  5  3  1
Library of Congress Cataloging-in-Publication Data
Pearlman, Bobby.
Leaf dance / by Bobby Pearlman ; illustrated by Kathryn Mitter.
p. cm. — (Ready-to-read) (Classic Raggedy Ann & Andy)
Summary: Raggedy Ann, Raggedy Andy, and the other toys throw a party
to celebrate the first day of fall.
ISBN 0-689-84679-7
[1. Dolls—Fiction. 2. Toys—Fiction. 3. Autumn—Fiction. 4. Parties—Fiction.]
I. Mitter, Kathy, ill. II. Title. III. Series. IV. Series: Classic Raggedy Ann & Andy
PZ7.P31658 Le 2001
[E]—dc21
2001029251

# Leaf Dance

by Bobby Pearlman
illustrated by Kathryn Mitter

Ready-to-Read

Little Simon
New York   London   Toronto   Sydney   Singapore

"It is the first day of fall!"

yelled Raggedy Andy.

"Let's have a party!"

The dolls went outside.

The air was cold.

It was a perfect fall day.

Fido barked and ran in circles.

He loved a party.

"Let's pick some apples,"

Raggedy Ann said.

So they did.

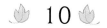

Raggedy Ann and the Camel with the

Wrinkled Knees saw a scarecrow.

The cold wind blew his arms and legs.

It looked like he was dancing!

Raggedy Andy saw the leaves

blowing.

"Let's have a leaf dance party!"

he said.

"May I come?" asked a big

orange pumpkin.

"I can not dance,

but I can decorate!" he said.

Raggedy Ann hugged Pumpkin.

"Of course you may come!" she said.

The dolls saw some Leaf Fairies.

"We are going to have a leaf dance,"

Raggedy Andy said.

"May we come?"

asked the Leaf Fairies.

"Yes, do come," Little Brown Bear said.

"Leaf dances are so much fun!"

The Leaf Fairies tickled a big tree.

The tree laughed

and her leaves floated down.

"Look," Raggedy Ann said.

"Each leaf is different."

One leaf was long, one was short,

some had points, and some were round.

 22

"Each leaf is a different color, too,"

said Raggedy Andy.

One leaf was brown, one was red,

some were yellow, and some were green.

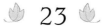

The Camel with the Wrinkled

Knees stepped on some leaves.

CRUNCH!

They smelled sweet!

Little Brown Bear gave each doll an apple.

Uncle Clem put Pumpkin next

to the big tree.

The dolls made a big pile of leaves.

Fido and Henny jumped into it.

"Whee!" the Leaf Fairies cried

as leaves floated down.

The leaves were dancing!

The dolls danced with them.

Uncle Clem danced with Frederika.

Raggedy Ann hugged Pumpkin.

Henny danced with Cleety the Clown.

Raggedy Andy and Little Brown Bear

spun around.

"I love the first day of fall!"

cheered Raggedy Andy.

"We love leaf dances!"

cried the Leaf Fairies and the dolls.

"And I love all of you!" said Raggedy Ann